MAMA GOD, PAPA GOD
A Caribbean Tale

by Richardo Keens-Douglas
illustrated by Stefan Czernecki

Crocodile Books, USA

An imprint of Interlink Publishing Group, Inc.
NEW YORK

Once upon a time — before my time, before your time, before anybody's time, even before there was time — Mama God and Papa God lived in the empty darkness.

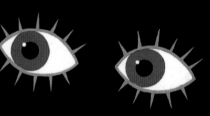

"Why are we sitting here in the dark?" Papa God wondered. All of a sudden, he lifted his hands way up high and said, "Let there be light."

Then he saw Mama God for the first time and smiled, "This is good. I can see how beautiful you are. Now I'm going to make something beautiful for you to see — something . . . round."

And Papa God made the world. Just like that!

Mama God looked at what he had made and said, "This is very good, but we should touch it up a bit."

So Papa God and Mama God set about filling the world with trees and flowers and animals and birds and water and fish and wind and rain. They set it spinning, so that there was day and night and, around it, they created the stars, the moon and the sun.

Oh, they made more wondrous things than you could ever name!

Mama God turned to Papa God and said, "I like looking at you, Papa. Why don't you put something that looks like you on the earth?"

"Like me? But what do I look like?" Papa God asked.

"Love, pure love!" she said with a gleam in her eye.

Papa God smiled. He looked down on the earth with love — and he made *man*.

"ow it's your turn, Mama God," he said.

Mama God gave a big belly laugh. She looked down on the earth with love—and she made *woman*.

Mama God started to get very excited. "Let's make a lot more of *man* and *woman* and call them *people*," she said.

So they began to make lots and lots of people.

Papa God was making people left, right, and center. Mama God thought he would never stop.

"That's enough Papa. That's enough!" she laughed. "We have to leave something for them to do, you know."

Mama God started to hum, which filled the earth with the sounds of wind and rain and animals and birds and insects.

Papa God loved listening to the music Mama God made.

And they both loved watching the many ways their children celebrated life.

Delighted with their work, they took a long stroll through the heavens.

Mama God was quiet for a long time.

Then she said, "I think the people should all be different from one another, like the birds and flowers."

"That's just what is needed!" agreed Papa God with a big grin.

And they set to work making all the people different.

Oh, the colors, the shapes, and the sizes they blessed the people with! Everyone different! Everyone beautiful! Everyone a masterpiece!

Papa God and Mama God scattered the people to all the corners of the earth. Then in each of those places Papa God gave the people a different language and dialect to speak.

"If everyone looked alike and spoke the same language, it would be very boring," he said. "This way they can live their lives learning all about each other."

Papa God and Mama God looked down on the world and agreed that it was truly a wonderful place.

Hand in hand, they strolled through the heavens creating more and more magnificent things.

For the future, for the new millenium
—R. K-D.

For Timothy Rhodes
—S. C.

First American edition published 1999 by

Crocodile Books, USA

An imprint of Interlink Publishing Group, Inc.
99 Seventh Avenue • Brooklyn, New York 11215 and
46 Crosby Street • Northampton, Massachusetts 01060

Published simultaneously in Canada and Great Britain by Tradewind Books Ltd.

Library of Congress Cataloging-in-Publication Data

Keens-Douglas, Richardo.
  Mama God, Papa God: A Caribbean tale / by Richardo Keens-Douglas;
  illustrated by Stefan Czernecki.
    p.   cm.
  Summary: Papa God creates light so that he can see Mama God, and then he makes
  the world because he wants to give her something beautiful.
  ISBN 1-56656-307-0
  1. Creation—Folklore.   2. Folklore—Caribbean Area.
  I. Czernecki, Stefan, ill.   II. Title
  PZ8.1.K26Mam   1999
  398.2'09729—dc21   98-38628
  [E]   CIP AC

Designed by Andrew Johnstone

Assistant to illustrator Michael Haijtink
Editorial assistance by Timothy Rhodes

Printed and bound in Hong Kong
10 9 8 7 6 5 4 3 2 1

To order or request our complete catalog,
please call us at **1-800-238-LINK**
or write to: